I am very lucky to be happily living in the countryside not too far from a good beach or two. I enjoy wild walks with my dogs on the south downs and watching my grandchildren ride along with spending time among the horses which has become a passion revisited.

To my amazing parents with love. Sylvie and Ken together
again xx
Moon and stars
Always Pants xxxx

LULU BEE

GREAT GATHERING CONKERS AND THE BLOSSOM TOP GANG

AUSTIN MACAULEY PUBLISHERS™

LONDON · CAMBRIDGE · NEW YORK · SHARJAH

A CIP catalogue record for this title is available from the British Library.

ISBN 9781528997836 (Paperback)
ISBN 9781528997843 (ePub e-Book)

www.austinmacauley.com

First Published 2022
Austin Macauley Publishers Ltd®
1 Canada Square
Canary Wharf
London
E14 5AA

Chapter One

'Come on, look to it. Up and Adam everybody,' said Grandma Beany.

'Jack and Callie will be arriving today.'

Loud giggles and belly chuckles started ringing out across the kitchen, along with the sound of glass bumping together, this caught Grandma's attention, so she looked around towards the shelves by the window.

'Oh, Mr Jar, do settle down or you will be tipping all your raspberries out,' she said. Mr Jar could hardly contain himself. He gets so excited when the grandchildren are coming, and excitement means lots of loud laughing. He rolled around on the shelf holding his tummy, bursting with thunder chuckles of delight. Grandma could see Mr Jar was soon to topple, and just as she was going to pick him up off the shelf, sure enough he tipped over, spilling his raspberries everywhere. Of course, he didn't notice, he was laughing far too much.

'Mr Jar!' cried Grandma, 'you really are very silly you know,' and all the other jars nodded in agreement. Sultana Jar, who is always very serious, raised her eyebrows right up to her rim and tut tutted very loudly. Mr Jar poked out his tongue at her, and immediately started to scream with laughter again.

'Honestly! How rude,' said Sultana Jar. Grandma Beany picked up Mr Jar, and placed him onto the table, where he continued to roar with laughter. Mrs Pot and Mr Pan were already on the table, so Grandma asked them to keep a firm eye on him. His laughter, by this time, had become so infectious that most of the kitchen had started to laugh too. Mrs Pot's giggling made her large copper bottom rattle and Mr Pan was making piggy oink sounds, trying to hold his laughter in. The spoons were squealing with giggles and the knives were playing bumper cars with each other and making themselves laugh even more. The forks were wiggling their prongs all over in a frenzy. Tommy Toaster kept popping his toasting racks up and down, and Ollie oven kept ringing his timing bell. Even the delicate, and very pretty, china cups were putting their handles to their mouths, trying desperately to stop the very loud and actually, very un-ladylike laugh that was coming from them. Very soon, Grandma was roaring with laughter too, so much so, she nearly fell off her chair. It did not help that the chair was also laughing so much; it was practically throwing Grandma off, which made her laugh even more as she desperately held on. The whole cottage was shaking with laughter. There was one though, who was not amused! That was Prunella Prickles, the large and beautiful ornate lamp on the sideboard, which was next to Rory, the rocking chair. Even he was rocking dangerously with laughter. Suddenly, Mr Applefield rushed in through the back door.

'Grandma Beany! Grandma Beany!' he cried. The whole kitchen went deadly quiet in a second, with all eyes wide, everyone looked at one another, and then at Mr Applefield.

'What's wrong?' said Grandma, standing up from her chair.

'Well,' boomed Mr Applefield in rather a rush. 'It's been brought to my attention that the Magic Meadow is in tears. In TEARS,' he boomed again.

'In tears? Oh my, what could be wrong?' asked Grandma, looking very concerned, yes, very concerned indeed. This had never happened before.

'Right everyone, back to your places, quick, quick, toot, toot. Mr Applefield, and I must go and investigate what's happened,' she said. The whole kitchen stayed very quiet with everyone looking at one another, now with worried looks, and all who could, hurried back to their places. The others would wait until Grandma Beany returned.

The garden watched as Grandma and Mr Applefield raced by. Gerald, the garden broom, stopped sweeping and wondered what an earth was going on. Simon, the garden spade went flying into the mud he was digging, as they shot past him.

'Sorry, Simon dear,' she called out.

Really! Sorry indeed! thought Simon. They ran through the Singing Rose Garden, and all the roses let out a beautiful,

'Ooh, ahhh!' as they went by.

'Beautiful, darlings, beautiful,' cried out Grandma, as they disappeared into the apple orchard. All the trees turned to one another,

'What's going on?' they all started asking. 'Where are they both going in such a hurry?'

They intended to race through butterfly row, which is the only way out of Blossom Top and the only way in, but the butterfly fairies had other ideas. They began to gather in huge numbers around them, and the more that came, the more Grandma and Mr Applefield tried to move fast unfortunately the fairies had already gained power and the spell had already be whispered making them move in slow motion. The glorious scent that the fairies blew out travelled up their noses, almost bringing them to a standstill. Grandma Beany mustered all her strength and gave Mr Applefield an almighty push, the fairies loved Mr Applefield he is their favourite, and Mr Applefield loved being whispered spells of sweet nothings, so they held firmly onto him. Grandma's nostrils began to quiver with delight, if ever there was a sign she had to move quicker, this was it. Therefore, filled with great urgency, she again found the strength to give Mr Applefield one last shove that was so hard, they both went rolling, and tumbling out of butterfly row landing in a big heap on top of one another. Mr Applefield lay there for a moment catching his breath, as did Grandma, both struggled to stand,

'Goodness gracious me!' she said. Mr Applefield looked up at her, and said rather breathlessly, 'Tumbling Tumble Weeds! I haven't done that for a while!' and they both laughed.

'Let's not forget why we fell, Mr Applefield,' Grandma said quickly. Mr Applefield got up, and they both started to run once more. Finally, they reached the magic meadow and, sure enough, there was much crying going on. Grandma Beany went over to the Daisy May girls, all of their beautiful petals were drooping, and all had little tears rolling down their tiny, sunshine yellow faces.

'Oh, my girls! My girls! What is the matter?' said Grandma. All the daisy mays started to speak at once,

'Oh Grandma,' said the tallest of them all, 'we were sleeping, when suddenly, it became very, very cold. So cold, our petal tips were starting to freeze, I mean, really freeze, until we could not feel them.'. 'We were so frightened,' squeaked the smallest one.

'Girls, girls, please do not cry. Where were the night beings, after all it is their job to protect you?' she asked in a very gentle voice.

'We don't know, we called out for them, but they didn't come.'

'Did you see anything or hear anything?' boomed Mr Applefield.

'Yes!' they all said. 'Strange and harsh sounding voices that said, soon we would all be gone, and that our magic meadow would be finished, and the criminals who are in daffadillion forever prisonwill be set free. Then there was lots of evil laughter, and they disappeared across the meadow, freezing everyone in their path. We could hear their screams, Grandma, it was awful!'

'Set free?' said Grandma, with tears in her own eyes. All the Daisy Mays began to nod their little flower tops in dismay.

Mr Applefield was scratching his head, trying to work out what on earth was going on, and where on earth had the night beings gone. He looked at Grandma and said in his big booming voice, 'This is a big worry, Grandma; the loss of the magic meadow would mean the end of Blossom Top, as we know it. Upside Wood would darken the whole land, all that is good will be gone.'

'You're quite right, Mr Applefield. You are quite right,' . Looking very sad, grandma turned back to the girls and assured them that the meadow would be kept safe and best news of all, the grandchildren were due to arrive any time today, and had now come of age.

'You know what that means, my darlings. The gang will be together again, soon.' All the Daisy Mays lifted their little flower tops and cried, 'Hooray! Hooray!' Mr Applefield and Grandma then walked, very carefully, over to the Dancing Dandelions.

'Oh, my dears! My dears!' she said, 'please don't cry.' The dancing dandelions all swayed miserably.

'Have the daisy mays told you what happened, Grandma.' They all asked while still sobbing.

'Yes, my dears, they have,' replied Grandma.

'Did you see, or hear, anything?' boomed Mr Applefield.

'No, not really, it just became very cold, very cold indeed, which woke us up. We were all shivering terribly, and we called for the night beings to ask why it was so cold, but they didn't come, and when dawn broke we saw the writing.'

'What writing my dears, where?'

'Over there,' and sure enough there was, frozen onto the mound around the meadow the words, RELEASE OUR FRIENDS OR WE WILL FREEZE THE MEADOW FOREVER;

'Good Lord!' said Grandma.

'Nothing for it! Nothing for it! This is a matter of urgency!' They are clearly talking about the daffodil folk, and that can never happen, Grandma, never!' Boomed Mr Applefield.

Grandma Beany turned back towards the dancing dandelions, and when she saw them, with their emerald green leaves resting on their golden yellow flower top faces, looking so frightened, she felt very hurt.

'There, there my darlings. Do not fear. We will make sure nothing happens to you all. My days of protecting Blossom Top have passed, and it is clear Upside Wood are aware of this, but, what they are not aware of, is that the grandchildren are on their way, and have come of age now, so the gang will be reunited once again.'

The dancing dandelions all let out tiny sighs of relief, and began to smile a smile, so bright, it shone like the sun on Grandma and Mr Applefield's faces.

After Grandma had assured the meadow all would be well, and they were not to be frightened anymore, the flowers began to look at one anotherbending and swaying. As Grandma and Mr Applefield began to walk away, a big ray of sunshine burned through the morning mist, causing the meadow to burst into song. It was so beautiful, it sounded like a million angels singing, magical for good people, deadly for bad! Grandma Beany and Mr Applefield stood with the lovely hot sun on their faces, listening to the meadow song, and watching as the flowers danced, and sang in the sunshine. It was so relaxing and warm, they could not move until the singing stopped.

'Thank goodness the children have come of age. It is not a moment too soon. It is for them to protect Blossom Top now, as I have done all these years. I can't wait to see what powers they have been given.'

On their way back to the cottage, Grandma Beany stopped in the orchard to bid the apple trees good morning, and to explain what had happened, and that there is now a mystery to be solved, and an adventure to be had, and the gang will all be together again soon, so hold on to your apples!'

All the apple trees pulled faces of uncertainty, as did their apples, upon them.

'What a palaver!' said the tallest of the trees, and all the trees shook their branches and started to talk amongst themselves.

'Did she say the flower meadow is under attack?' asked one.

'Yes! Oh, yes! It could be us next!' screamed the apples, with eyes as wide as tea saucers.

'Okay! Everyone.' said the tallest tree, 'we are officially on, 'Far and Wide' alert!'

All the apple trees lifted their branches up as high as they would go, into the far and wide lookout position. The little apples were rather nervous, 'It is an awfully long way down!

What if we suddenly become ripe, and fall?' The bravest of the apples spoke up, voicing his concerns to his tree.

'Now, look here tree, it's a long way down from here, should I ripen and fall?' His tree gave him a cross wasp kind of look, and began to shake his branches, while singing loudly, 'Shake rattle and roll! I say shake rattle and roll!'

'Arrrghhh! Okay, okay. You win,' said the little apple. His tree gave him a nod and a wink and stopped.

Grandma and Mr Applefield had now reached the entrance to butterfly row.

'After three,' Grandma said. Mr Applefield nodded.

'One, Two, Three, go!' she cried. Both ran as fast as they could. The butterfly fairies started gathering around them once again. This time, loudly whispering their sweet nothings. Grandma and Mr Applefield began to move in slow motion, so they stopped moving, and stood quite still to trick the fairies into thinking they had given up. The fairies stopped too, and all was strangely still for a moment.

'Run!' cried Grandma. The unsuspecting fairies were too slow to catch on, as Grandma and Mr Applefield raced to the end. 'Few ee!' said Grandma. They eventually, made it back into the kitchen, where everyone was awaiting news.

Chapter Two

'Well, it seems we have rather a mystery on our hands,' Grandma said. The whole kitchen gasped and started to chatter all at the same time. They all stopped when Mr Apple field boomed, 'Yes, it's a pretty serious situation make no mistake,' he said, while shaking his head from side to side, releasing a big mop of hair onto his very bushy eyebrows, which covered his big red nose and very red cheeks. Prunella Prickles looked up from under her shade and said to Rory Rocking Chair in her la de da tone,

'Well, at least this will keep the grandchildren outside and away from me.'

'Prunella dear,' called out Grandma, 'behave yourself.'

'Well really!' huffed Prue, feeling embarrassed and deciding she was definitely going to bite anyone who dared to switch her on, especially the grandchildren.

'Mr Applefield, would you care for a teapot tea? I think we could both do with one, don't you?'

'Jolly, good idea! I say,' boomed Mr Applefield, smiling from ear to ear at the thought of one of Grandma's tea pot teas, but before Grandma Beany could even fill the pot with tea leaves, through the back door came running Jack and Callie, and the whole kitchen erupted into uproar.

'Grandma!' they both shouted and ran to hug her.

'Oh, my darlings,' said Grandma as they all hugged and squeezed one another. While all this hugging and squeezing was going on, Barney Biscuit Barrel moved into position with a huge smile on his face, these were the moments he lived for waiting to be emptied of all Grandma's homemade biscuits.

'You won't get far with your biscuits today while I'm about, Barney,' Timothy Cake Tin said. Barney Biscuit Barrel just huffed and turned the other way as Grandma had told him to do.

'Oh, the tea! My dears,' said Grandma. Everyone let go of one another and they all sat down. They all drank and ate lots of cake and biscuits, while laughing and talking.

From the corner of her eye, Callie could see Digby Door Soldier standing in the hallway with his head hanging low.

Digby is a smashing little door soldier. He wears a very impressive soldier's uniform with a shiny black hat and the reddest little jacket with the biggest and shiniest gold buttons you ever did see. He had on very smart black trousers and such shiny boots, you can see yourself in them.

'Ahh, Digby!' said Callie. 'What's the matter?' Digby raised his head and looked at her with such large sad eyes; she immediately got down from the table and ran over to him. Callie kneeled on the floor and gave him a huge cuddle. When Callie finally let him go, he marched around and around in circles saying, 'Welcome home! Giggerdy gig! Welcome home! Giggerdy gig!' Then he marched straight to the front door.

'Grandma, what's wrong with Digby?' asked Callie.

'Oh, dear goodness me!' said Grandma. 'What with all the excitement I'd forgotten about poor Digby! Children, you came in the back door and Digby has been waiting all morning for you at the front door.'

'No problem,' said Jack, 'come on, Callie,' and Callie followed Jack out of the back door.

'Jack wait, slow down. Where are we going?' shouted Callie.

'Round to the front door, Silly!' He shouted back. The very large brass old man knocker with his big bushy beard gave them both a large toothless smile in appreciation after Jack had knocked his knocker loudly. On the other side of the door in the hallway, Digby instantly stood to attention.

'About turn! Giggerdy gig!' he shouted and began to march to the front door.

'Quick march, Digby! You are needed,' called out Grandma, 'remember to keep the children away from the

18

stairs when they come in.' Digby smiled a huge smile and began to turn the handle at the bottom of the door that Grandma had made for him. He turned with all his might until the door opened.

'Hello Digby,' cried Jack and Callie together.

'Jiggerdy jig! jiggerdy jig! Well, how do you do? Jiggerdy jig! Jiggerdy jig! So pleased to see you,' shouted Digby. The children came in through the door and marched with Digby to the kitchen, both smiling at one another.

'Well done, Digby,' said Grandma, 'thank you so much for letting the children in.'

'Yes, thank you, Digby,' they both said. Callie bent down and gave Digby another big hug and a kiss on his cheek. He was so delighted; his little cheeks went bright red as he marched back to his favourite chair in the living room.

'Now children, we have a mystery to solve and another adventure to be had and as you know it is all up to you two now.'

'Great Gathering Conkers! What is it?,' asked Jack and before anyone could answer him The Great Gathering Conkers began to appear on each of Jack's shoulders.

Conkernaid was the first out. He jumped onto the kitchen table and with both hands on his hips he looked around at everyone nodding his head,

'Yep, it's me. I'm here.'

'He's here! He's here!' swooned the SP00NETS

Conkernaid's specialist combat skill is to land and explode on the target. He can run as fast as a cheetah, explode and walk away unharmed, leaving the villain covered in warm sticky Conker mush which dries like concrete in seconds. Mr Jar was amazed at the sight of Conkernaid. He had an urge to throw raspberries at him, but thought better of it. Conkernaid put on his shades and ripped open his shirt, puffed out his chest while looking at Prunella and winking; Pru's lampshade turned bright red.

'Really! For goodness sake!' she said with her shade bowed down. Conkernaid then turned to Jack and said, 'At yer service.'

19

'Wow!' screamed the Spoonets and all passed out!

Next, to appear was Spikey Conk. He raced out like a wild Conker, summersaulted onto the table, and in the blink of an eye appeared his large silver spikes; the very sharp and pointed ends glistened in the kitchen light. Everyone shuddered; Spikey Conk, never quite comes out of his shell as his specialist combat skills are one, working as an undercover spy, and two, being able to fire his spikes with red hot accuracy pinning the villain down with such force they are unable to move an inch. He threw up his hands and waved at everyone, and in his deep Scottish tones said, 'At yee service, Jack,' before lining up next to Conkernaid. The whole kitchen waited in anticipation and then, BOOM! And from behind a dazzling flash of light appeared Electra Conk! He looked around at everyone. The Spoonets all put their tiny hands onto their hearts and sighed. Electra Conk gave them a wink, flashed another bolt of lightning, and said, 'Hello ladies, may I say you are looking particularly beautiful today.' The Spoonets all passed out yet again.

Electra Conk's combat skill is target perfect lightning strikes, after throwing some bolts around the kitchen and making everyone jump, especially Jack, he got in line.

Then came Ultra Conk, the largest and meanest of conkers. Ultra-Conk took no prisoners. He had on a suit of armour and no villain ever escaped a crushing experience in just one of his huge hands if they got in his way. He jumped onto the table with an almighty bang, shaking the table and looked around menacingly. The whole kitchen tried to avoid his gaze.

Then it was the turn of Cool Conk, dressed in a white suit he swaggered onto the table nodding and winking at all the ladies in the room. Cool Conk's specialist combat skill is freezing the enemy, solid. Captain Conk was out next. He stood and gave Jack a salute. Captain Conk's specialist combat skill is being a leader of men.

'Okay, everyone, line up, line up,' said Captain Conker, 'line up, I say! Are all conkers present and correct?'

'Yes sir.'

'No Sir!' called out Ultra Conk.

'Who's missing?' asked Captain Conk.

'Booga Conk, sir,' said Conkernaid.

Booga Conk! What the heck? thought Mr Jar to himself?

'Ta Dah! Here I am! Ready or not! Boogas you want, well boogas, I've got.'

'No!' screamed the Spoonets 'Please, what are boogas?' they squealed.

' bogies, you dollies', said Mr Jar. TheSpoonets yet again performed the passing out parade and all collapsed.

Bogies! How very disgusting! thought Prunella?

Booga Conk just stood still watching everyone from one eye with a cheeky smile on his face.

'What can we do for ya, Jack?' asked Captain Conker. Jack sat quietly in amazement at what had just happened; after all, he had never met the Great Gathering Conkers before and had never even said great gathering conkers before he was overwhelmed at their powers (his powers)! Grandma, sensing Jack's surprise turned to him and said, 'These are the gifts you have been given to protect Blossom Top, Jack. Use them wisely, but for now thank them and tell them it was a pleasure to meet them, and you will call again when you need them.' Jack did just that.

'Quick march then back to barracks, hup two three four.' shouted Captain Conker and they all marched back to Clobbernut, but before he disappeared, Booga Conk turned suddenly holding one nostril as if to fire livebogies at someone. The bogies loved to wrap their thick green sticky lumpy selves around anyone they landed on they always aimed for the mouth and tried to get in. The whole kitchen screamed and took cover. Booga conk laughed and was gone.

'Well, Jack, it seems you have been blessed with an impressive bunch for your powers,' said Grandma. When all in the kitchen had settled down from all the excitement and the Spoonets had recovered, Grandma started to tell the children what had happened that morning. Jack and Callie listened, as did all who were present. There were lots of ums and ahhs and raised eyebrows.

'Well,' said Jack, and everyone turned to look at him. At this, Prunella Prickles just raised her eyes up to her lampshade, 'Oh, dear here we go, kerfuffle and nonsense over nothing,' she said.

'Really Prue, you know Jack and Callie are the new protectors of our home,' said Rory the Rocking Chair.

'Oh please,' she replied, 'I will still try to bite them if they dare to switch me on!'

'Well, children, what do you think?' asked Grandma. Jack looked at Callie and then they both looked at Grandma.

'I say, let us go and see what is going on,' he said.

Chapter Three

The whole kitchen roared with hoorays and shouts of excitement. The spoons, well nothing could stop them from squealing loudly over just about everything. Mr Jar could not contain his excitement and as usual fell off the shelf spilling his raspberries everywhere! The whole cottage vibrated with the noise.

'Calm down, everyone please,' called out Grandma.

'I think we are going to have to ask the Spindle Webs for help. Maybe if we ask them nicely, they can cast their webs over the meadow and keep it safe until we catch the criminal, or criminals who are doing this,' said Jack. Callie gasped at this news and the poor spoons squeaked with horror and all, yep you've guessed it,' passed out once again. Mr Jar's eyes popped out so far, they hit the ceiling and sprang back into their sockets with such force he fell backwards spilling even more raspberries. This made Sultana Jar laugh so much she wobbled almost falling off the shelf herself and made all the other jars laugh at her.

'Not funny,' she sulked.

'Mm,' said Grandma Beany, 'the Spindle Webs are a tricky bunch, Jack.'

'That they are,' boomed Mr Applefield.

'Tricky bunch, don't you mean, sticky bunch,' said Prunella and laughed so much her shade fell off. It wasn't often anyone saw Prunella laugh, let alone loose her shade, the whole kitchen looked around at one another frowning and pulling faces, then fell about laughing. Grandma walked over to Prue and tidied her up.

'Do you realise, Prunella, you just made a kind of joke,' said Callie.

'Hum,' said Prue, feeling very silly.

'Best we get to it then,' said Grandma, 'we have a long journey ahead of us.'

'Yes,' said Jack, 'the Spindle Webs can only be found in Upside Wood and that's a long way off.'

The adventure begins.

All four set off in earnest, Jack, Callie, Grandma and Mr Applefield. First, they came to the Singing Rose Garden where all the roses raised their heads mischievously,

'Mm,' said one, 'where are you off to?'

'Upside Wood,' answered Jack.

'Ooooooo!' came the reply; all the roses looked at one another and started to sing very loudly, fluttering their eyelashes and just the tiniest slithers of what looked like smoke started to appear.

'Laughing gas,' said Grandma. 'We have to rush now! Come on everybody.'

'Ole!' sighed all the roses and watched them go.

'Ah', said Mr Applefield, 'Butterfly Row, we cannot be stuck here. We will have to run and run fast, so much time and so little to do,' he boomed.

'I think you meant to say that the other way around, Mr Applefield,' said Callie looking at him.

Butterfly row is a very long corridor, which you may or may not get to the end of. The beautiful fairy butterflies hypnotize you whispering their sweet nothings into your ears. Stand still for too long and it will be the walled garden for you, where your dreams good or bad come true, the way back is then closed, and you will never get through, though some do! These fairy butterflies are a treat to your eyes and a glorious gift to the nose; their scent comes from your happy place. Their wings are the colour gold and glisten in the sun. They feel like feathers brushing past you. They swarm around you in their thousands so that you can feel their sweet blossom breathe on your face. Their tiny hands are just about visible to the naked eye and their tiny delicate bodies are as light as a snowflake. Their beautiful little round faces and tiny black eyes look into yours as they gently hypnotize. They touch your hair and kiss you lightly. You feel so happy and warm as they lift you off your feet, all your worries disappearing as they take you with them deep into blossom earth from where you will return only in your dreams, so be swift my dears through Butterfly Row as nothing is quite what it seems.

Jack was the first to reach the row and raced through like grease lightning.

'Come on,' he shouted. Everyone was still at the entrance.

'Okay, I think we should all hold hands and run through as quick as we can,' said Grandma.

'Okay,' agreed Callie.

'Here, here,' boomed Mr Applefield, 'so much time and so little to do,' he said again. Callie just looked at him and shook her head and Grandma smiled. The smell was already becoming glorious to the nose and it was already making their nostrils quiver. With the sun blistering down onto the thousands of sparkling wings, it became hard to see.

'We must be sure not to anger them or hurt them as we run through,' said Grandma.

'Right ho,' said everyone, and they began to run. The butterfly fairies were everywhere, all around them, touching their faces and whispering in their ears, but with so many of them the whispering became louder and each person could no longer see in front of them. All were becoming more and more disorientated.

'Come, come with us, come with us my dears,' they whispered. Everyone started to run in slow motion everything got slower and slower, like running in treacle.

'Keep going,' called Grandma. Mr Applefield seemed to be having great problems, after all this was amongst one of his most favourite places, which he visited quite often for a dose of happiness. Once, he was gone for months, funny though they always let him go. He had lost his grip of Callie's hand and fallen rather behind. The butterfly fairies began to concentrate just on him. Callie and Grandma were able to speed up again and managed to reach the end, huffing and puffing like steam trains.

'Golden Goshes!' said Callie, and with that, a sparkling halo of light rose above her head. Her hair was sucked upwards and whirled around like a tornado and from out of it came tiny, but very fat angry looking babies who gathered above her head with harps and started to sing. Jack looked at Grandma, mouth agape and eyes wide.

'What?' was the only word to come out of his mouth? 'Just weird,' he said and started to laugh.

'Not half as weird as your conkers,' said Callie giving him a shove. This made the fat babies laugh so much their heads came clean off, not a good look really, fat babies with no heads! 'Oh, dear this isn't good,' said Callie, as two of their little heads floated in front of her face giggling.

'Gross!' said Jack. Callie composed herself as best she could even though her shock and amazement had made her tremble all over. She knew she had to control the situation and asked the fat babies to gather their heads and leave, which they did much to Jack's amusement and Callie's relief.

'Interesting,' Grandma said, 'I am eager to see what your little guys are capable of, Callie,' she added.

'So am I, Grandma,' Callie said, unsure of her newly acquired powers. They all waited and waited for Mr Applefield.

'Oh, dear we may have lost him,' said Grandma. Then suddenly, and at considerable speed he came rolling along the ground, covered in leaves and dirt glowing from head to foot with a huge smile on his very red face.

'Didn't think I would make it!' he boomed, 'did not know if I even wanted to!' he boomed again. Everyone laughed. They continued their journey down the lane and into the orchard, of course all the trees and the apples upon them knew they were coming this time, since they were all in the far and wide lookout position.

'Hello, hello,' they all started calling at once. The little apples were swinging around giggling and laughing at the sight of the grandchildren.

'Hello, hello,' they all called.

'Hi, everyone,' Jack called back.

'Hi,' said Callie. The trees were toing and froing so much it was causing quite a breeze, which was very welcome on such a hot day. Once through the orchard, it was only a bit further on to the most beautiful, most magical and most deadly, for criminals only, flower meadow.

Once the meadow saw Jack and Callie had arrived, the excitement was enormous. Swaying and singing rippled across the huge expanse before them; it was truly awesome, and the only piece of land standing between good and bad, the only protection from Upside Wood and all its foul criminal inhabitants. Jack and Callie watched for a moment, and then made their way towards the daisy mays to tell them of their plans to find the freeze that had invaded the meadow the night before. They spoke to the dancing dandelions and all concerned. While talking Callie felt something pulling at her trouser leg and looked down to see, a stone.

'Yes, yes, it's me pulling at you,' it said.

'Really?' said Callie.

'Yes, I know I'm just a little stone. We are all just little stones,' and all of a sudden, a circle of faces was looking up at her.

'Wow,' said Callie, 'how cute!'

'Pardon?' said Jack, looking around towards her.

'Look at these little chaps, Jack!' He looked down to see the stones smiling up at him.

They had huge teeth! Creepy! thought Jack. The stones introduced themselves:

'We are the stones. Yeah that is right! No special name, just the stones.' Jack and Callie looked at each other and both said together, 'Pleased to meet you, stones.'

'Likewise, we have been eager to meet you,' said the stones.

'Really?' said Jack, and before anymore could be said, all the stones rolled away.

'Wait!' Callie called after them, but they were gone. Jack turned back to the dancing dandelions, who told them both, that to see the stones meant Upside Wood and all who lived there now knew that the children were here. Callie looked at

Jack with a concerned expression and both wondered if this was a good or a bad thing? They must ask Grandma. Once they were back across the meadow to where Grandma and Mr Applefield were sitting, Callie told them both about the stones.

'Not good! Not good at all!' boomed Mr Applefield.

'They know you're here now,' said Grandma.

'You must be on your guard. Those were the Clones' stones, they will try to help you, but they are a cowardly bunch and could turn against you at a click of the fingers, so don't be fooled.'

Unbeknown to them all, behind a large tuft of grass was hiding a stingle, these are curious and mischievous creatures who live in Upside Wood. They are as small as leprechauns and just as green, clothed in nettles, in fact, no one really knows if the nettle leaves are their clothes or their bodies! They have very cross looking little faces with a very pointy nose and eyes like marbles with orange centres, and they can move as quick as a flash. They hide very well and have excellent hearing, and a fearsome sting. In fact, they are all together quite unpleasant and jolly spiteful. This particular stingle listened carefully to what everyone was saying, and then crept away.

The journey begins.

Meanwhile, back in the kitchen everyone was waiting in anticipation for some news.   . The spoons were as always, practicing their dance moves up and down the kitchen worktop. With their hands on their hips, they were doing a dance called the 'One step sway.' Which consisted of sway to your left one-step, sway to your right one-step,

'La la, de, de, come dance with me,' they all sang while admiring themselves in each other's reflection; something they did very well.

'Hoorah! Hoorah!' shouted Tommy Toaster.

'Bravo!' yelled Ollie Oven, and the whole kitchen began to clap. The spoons swivelled and swirled even more, making their shiny selves move to the beat of their song. The only one not clapping was Prunella Prickles.

'Oh, please they are only spoons!' she complained.

'Yes, and you are only a lamp,' shouted Mr Jar, and the whole kitchen roared with laughter.

'Well, really!' snorted Prue. The Spoonets had not heard Prue; they were all too busy showing off their dancing and singing skills.

'La, la, de, de, come dance with me,' they continued. Then Mr Jar shouted, 'I can juggle my raspberries! Want to see?' So everyone turned to watch. The Spoonets stopped and sat down, as did the knives who had been daring each other to fall off the kitchen side, and onto the floor and bounce back up again. The forks, on the other hand, were too busy having prong locking tournaments and would stop for no one. Mr Jar prepared himself. He cleared his throat and then made sure he had his balance and proceeded to juggle. The trouble with Mr Jar is he gets over excited with everything.

'Oh, yeah, oh, yeah! Look at me,' he shouted while wiggling and jiggling so rumbumptiously, his raspberries bounced up and down wildly. Sultana Jar was shaking her head from side to side in dismay, while the other jars began to snigger amongst themselves. Mrs Pot and Mr Pan were starting to snigger too. The whole kitchen watched as Mr Jar was tipping raspberries everywhere and laughing at himself for doing so. Olli Ovens timing bell started to ring, which made Prunella Prickles jump. She tutted and shook her shade so angrily it fell off! She screamed, 'My shade! My shade has fallen clean Orff!' With this, the whole kitchen just fell to pieces with laughter.

Back at the meadow, everyone had decided to return to the cottage and leave early in the morning to find the spindle webs, but they had one problem, who was going to guard the meadow tonight? now the night beings had mysteriously disappeared. What could they do? Grandma knew there was only one thing for it, she must use her final power, after all, this was a great emergency indeed and would mean the end of Blossom Top and all that is good if anything happened to the Magic Meadow. She had to think, and think fast, what would protect against freezing?

'Heat, of course,' she said aloud.

'What? Grandma,' said Jack. Callie just looked and Mr Applefield smiled; he knew Grandma had one last power left.

'Heat, my dears. We can protect the meadow tonight with heat,' said Grandma.

'How?' said Callie. 'I'll show you. Stand back, children,' she said. Grandma walked to the start of the Meadow and standing very still, she closed her eyes and started to meditate.

'Ricklespin, ricklespun, grant me my last one. Make it heat. Make it vast. Make it the night to last!' The sun turned swiftly in her direction, immediately her face went bright red, the sun then started to spin wildly. The children could not move nor could Mr Applefield. There was an invisible force holding them tightly to the spot. In the distance, coming towards them, they could see pink clouds; hundreds of them travelling at frightening speed. Everyone was hit with a wall of hot air which would have blown them away, had they not all been stuck to the ground. The clouds swirled around Grandma and then around the Meadow completely covering it, so all that was visible was a pink fluffy glow that seemed to stretch for miles. The sun stopped spinning, looked at Grandma, who seemed to be saying something to it, but no one could hear what, she then turned and walked back towards them all with a face as red as a tomato.

'Hoorah! Hoorah indeed!' boomed Mr Applefield.

'Wow! Grandma. What was that?' said Jack.

'Yes, what was that?' repeated Callie.

'That, my darlings, was the calling of the speckled moon desert wind! It will protect the meadow until whichever we find first, the criminals who are doing this, or the Spindle Webs. My powers are now no more, so it is up to you, children,' she said, 'but for now let's get back and begin again tomorrow.' All four made their way back to the cottage to eat and sleep. The next morning the sun was shining, and everyone was up at dawn. Grandma slid down the bannister, as usual, and the children copied; no point using the stairs as the carpet devils would be way too much to deal with first thing.

Breakfast was hearty and the whole cottage was alive with chatter in every room. After tea pot tea it was time for Mr Applefield to inform the children of the journey that lay ahead of them.

'The path to Upside Wood,' he began, 'lays across two farms. The first being, Crumble Farm and the second Tumbleweed Farm,' he boomed.

'Yes,' said Grandma, 'if, and when, you get across Tumbleweed farm there lies the rookery bridge, which is the entrance to Upside Wood.'

Crumble Farm belongs to Mrs Crumble; a very plump and rather scary looking lady with large round rosy cheeks, frizzy orange hair, bright red lipstick applied rather badly to her lips, huge teeth and large black bushy eyebrows. Every bush and every fence around Crumble Farm has bells on them millions of tiny bells. This is so Mrs Crumble never misses a visitor.

'Children, Mrs Crumble is the kindest dearest lady. She loves you to visit but hates you to leave.'

'Really?' said Jack 'Is that bad?' he asked.

'Yes, in a way, it is,' boomed Mr Applefield. 'The problem,' he continued, 'with Mrs Crumble is that she will feed you and feed you and feed you and with one taste of her crumble pie, you will happily want to keep eating and eating until you get so large, you can't move!'

'Great Gathering Conkers!' said Jack, and before you could blink an eye, Captain Conker appeared.

'Do you need us, sir?' he said to Jack.

'Erm, no, thank you. I think we are okay at the moment,' said Jack.

'Right, you are,' said Captain Conk and quietly retreated. Jack asked how they were going to get across Crumble Farm without setting the bells off.

'I've thought of that,' said Grandma, 'and there's nothing for it, Mr Applefield and I will have to tell her that we have come specially to have a slice of crumble pie and a cup of tea with her. Mr Applefield's face lit up, he loved crumble pie. There was one time he visited Crumble Farm and did not stop eating for three weeks. It would have been more, had Mrs

Crumble not fallen asleep at her stove and stopped baking. He remembered well, how he had become enormous and had great trouble moving, but move he had to, so he crawled all the way home. It took him months to recover, but all the same, he rather enjoyed it. Grandma Beany laughed when she looked at his face, as she herself had been stuck at Crumble Farm once before and knew very well the pleasure of eating crumble pie.

'Oh, Grandma, what will we do? You could be stuck at Crumble Farm for days, months, even years,' said Callie looking all concerned.

'Do not worry, my dear, we will be fine. Larger maybe, but fine.'

Chapter Four

They reached Crumble Farm and stopped at the fence.

'Golden Goshes!' said Callie and before you could say 'Bing bong! Let's have a song,' the sparkling halo of light surrounded Callie's head bringing with it the invisible tornado of wind, which whipped up her hair from which the fat babies appeared to the sound of harps, all cute and looking rather pleased with themselves. The others looked on in amazement. Grandma Beany marvelled at it. Mr Applefield loved the fat babies, but every time he went to touch them, they tried to bite him as for Jack; well, he still thought it was just plain weird.

'Not now! Please,' Callie said, so all the babies, there are four in all, started to wail. Their little faces turning red with anger they began firing flaming arrows aimlessly; Jack, Grandma and Mr Applefield took cover. Grandma shouted over to Callie, 'Take control, my dear. You must.'

'Stop it!' Callie shouted at the top of her voice. The fat babies looking really cross stopped firing their flaming arrows and retreated.

'Look at all the bells,' Callie finally got around to saying. In the sunlight, the whole of the farm twinkled with the tiny bells and in the middle was the cottage covered in what looked like cake!

'Grandma is that cake on the walls?' asked Jack.

'Of course!' boomed Mr Applefield, 'and jolly tasty it is too.'

'Okay, both of you. When the bells go off, Mrs Crumble will race from her cottage towards us laughing and trying to gather us all in. Mr Applefield and I will distract her from you, but you must run and run like blazes before you smell the crumble pie, she has more than one way of making you go with her.' Both Jack and Callie looked at Grandma and said, 'Right ho, Grandma.'

'Mr Applefield, before we part with them, please tell the children what they must do next.'

'Now then, listen carefully,' he boomed. 'Once you have climbed over the Crumble Farm fence over yonder, you will see two trees; you must walk through them,' he said.

'Remember, through them and not around them,' warned Grandma.

'Before you go through the two trees, call the name Skipperty loudly, and wait,' said Mr Applefield.

'Is that a rabbit?' asked Callie.

'You'll see, you'll see,' he replied.

'Once you're through, you will come upon Tumbleweed Farm which belongs to Farmer Wibberly. 'It's a beautiful farm full of the tallest and most yellow sunflowers you will ever see,' said Grandma, 'but beware, all is not what it appears.' She added, 'You must get across the farm before the rooks see you and wake Farmer Wibberly.'

'If they do, you will need all the help from Skipperty that you can get,' boomed Mr Applefield. With everyting having been explained they all pushed through the bushes and rightly enough, the bells started to ring. It was so loud they could not hear themselves think, let alone hear each other. They all started to run, and as was said, in the distance they could see Mrs Crumble running towards them. She was running like a mad thing with her hair all over the place and wearing large slippers, and even larger baggy socks.

'Run! You two! Run!' shouted Grandma Beany at the top of her voice. Jack grabbed Callie's hand tightly and took off towards the other side of the farm. Mrs Crumble saw this and started in their direction. Mr Applefield called after her, but she did not stop and kept running after Jack and Callie, who both by now could feel their noses starting to grow in the direction of the crumble pie smell,

'Jack! My nose!' Callie cried, while holding it and trying to stop it from growing.

'Just hold on, Callie!' Jack shouted back and held her hand even tighter and ran even faster.

Mrs Crumble was hot on their heels. Grandma and Mr Applefield were hot on Mrs Crumble's heels with noses as long as broom handles they were finding it hard to keep up,

'Do something, Mr Applefield!' shouted Grandma.

'We're so hungry,' cried out Mr Applefield, as loud as he possibly could, and Mrs Crumble came to a sudden stop and turned back towards him.

'Tut, tut! Naughty, naughty!' she said. 'Letting two get away! Well, you will just have to eat their share, Follow me.'

Grandma and Mr Applefield entered the cottage and the door closed with a bang behind them. Jack and Callie safely reached the other side of Crumble Farm and luckily, both their noses had shrunk back to their normal size. They scrambled through the bush and fell onto the grass sitting there a while to catch their breath.

'Oh, Jack, Grandma and Mr Applefield, I do hope they will be alright.'

'I'm sure they will be,' Jack replied, 'and if not, we will rescue them on the way back. Look there'sthe two trees, Callie, look over there.'

Callie looked around and sure enough, there they were. *How strange,* she thought to herself, *there seemed to be nothing else, but the grass they were sitting on the sky and the two trees.*

'Jack, does this look strange to you? I mean, I cannot see anything else; no farm, no fields no other trees, anything. It is as if we are on an island surrounded by sky instead of sea.' Jack looked around too.

'Yes, very strange,' he said. 'Have you had enough rest now, Callie?' he asked.

'Yes, thanks,' she replied.

'Then let's do what Mr Applefield told us to do, let's call Skipperty!' said Jack.

'Ah, yes let's. I cannot wait to see him. I bet he is a rabbit; a beautiful white rabbit like in Alice in Wonderland,' said Callie.

'Could be,' said Jack, thinking that was such a girl thing to say and smiling at his sister for having such whimsy thoughts, typical! 'Let's shout out loud together for Skipperty, ready?' Jack asked. They stood up brushed themselves off and shouted at the tops of their voices.

'Skipperty!,' and again 'Skipperty!' They stood waiting and waiting, and looking around, then, 'Did you hear that?' said Jack.

'Yes,' replied Callie, 'it sounded like a whistle.'

'There it is again, it's coming from behind one of the trees, I'm sure.' Jack said. 'Let's go over to the trees.'

'Do you think it's Skipperty?' asked Callie.

'There's only one way to find out. Callie, lets go.' They both started to make their way over to the trees, but stopped suddenly and watched, as from behind one of them came a large white, 'Hedgehog!'. They both said at the same time, while looking at one another then back at Skipperty.

'Are you Skipperty?' Callie asked, with a very quizzical look on her face.

'Yep, that's me, Skipperty Spikes at your service.' Suddenly, he stood up on his hind legs and was super tall.

'Wow!' said Jack.

'Surprised, isn't ya?' said Skipperty, while pulling out one of his very large spikes and using it as a tooth pick, winking at Callie at the same time. 'You both ready to walk through these trees then?' asked Skipperty. Before they could answer he said, 'Well, you can't go that way or this way, in fact no other way, but through the trees, otherwise you'll fall off.'

'Fall off what?' Callie asked.

'Why, the world, of course,' Skipperty said.

'You can't fall off the world,' said Jack.

'You can here,' said Skipperty, 'go, have a look for yourselves.' He moved his hand around and they both went to have a look, walking quickly towards the edge of the grass. 'Slowly, if I was you,' said Skipperty, and right enough when they both reached the edge, that was it, there was no more ground, just sky!

'Great Gathering Conkers!' cried Jack and as quick as a wick on a candle stick Captain Conk appeared, 'Are we needed, Jack?'

'Erm, no, but before you go look at this,' he said. Captain Conk took a quick look over the edge.

'Hey lads, get a load of this,' he shouted back to Clobbernut. With an impressive summersault, came conkernaid, rubbing his chin he looked around, did some karate moves and looked over the edge.

'Outstanding! Do we need ropes? SIR!' he said.

'Not right now, son, we are just observing the territory,' said the Captain.

Electra Conk and Ultra Conk were already out and looking around nodding their heads and discussing tactics. Cool Conk arrived shades on, looking, yep you guessed it, very cool. He looked over the edge and had a little laugh to himself, then spotted Callie and removed his shades, smiled and winked.

Booga Conk came rolling out last and looking around at the others nodding, he strolled over to the edge, looked down and smiled to himself. He held one side of his nostril closed and blew out two bogies from the other! Out they came, all green slimy and lumpy, and ready to attach themselves to someone, but instead they were looking into thin air, holding tightly onto one another they screamed as they fell. Booga Conk let out a loud and menacing laugh.

'Okay lads, now we know a tiny bit of what we are up against, we can return and get ready for the rest.'

'Yes, Sir,' they all said, and bidding Jack farewell, returned to Clobbernut. Skipperty Spikes had been watching all of this over by the trees.

'Friends of yours then, the conkers,' he said with a little smile on his face. 'I can see how they would be 'elpful in a crisis,' he added, and laughed. Callie saw Jacks face go red and looking just a little cross.

'I'll have, you know,' she said, 'The Great Gathering Conkers are Jacks new power and are a jolly tough lot.'

'Take no notice of him, Callie. Let us go back over to the trees,' said Jack.

'Right ho, Jack,' and they both walked back towards Skipperty.

Chapter Five

Back at Crumble Farm Grandma Beany and Mr Applefield were really starting to struggle with their seventh helping of crumble pie and custard. Mr Applefield's cheeks had become cherry bright he also had to undo several buttons here and there on his clothing. Grandma Beany was simply full to bursting point and Mrs Crumble was still talking while making more pie and stirring more custard.

'I wonder how the grandchildren are getting along,' Grandma whispered to Mr Applefield. He looked up from his bowl and whispered,

'I'm sure Skipperty will look after them.'

'I'm sure he'll clash with Jack too,' whispered Grandma.

'Well, that's something they will have to work out between them if they want to survive,' whispered Mr Applefield with his very serious face on.

'Indeed, Mr Applefield, indeed,' whispered Grandma. She once again picked up her spoon and went to put another piece of pie in her mouth, when suddenly an idea came to her on how they could escape. She nudged Mr Applefield who looked up from eating, Grandma gave him a little wink of her eye, and Mr Applefield knew that meant Grandma had, had one of her ideas, probably on how they were going to escape. *Oh, thank goodness, thank goodness,* he thought, *he really could not eat another mouthful, not this time anyway.* Grandma Beany lent over the table and whispered to Mr Apple field.

'I'll ask you something and you answer me quite loudly, so Mrs Crumble will hear.'

'Right ho,' replied Mr Applefield. So, Grandma whispered, 'I wonder where the grandchildren are.'

'Yes, yes we should look for them,' boomed Mr Applefield. Mrs Crumble turned around and said, 'Look for who?'

'Oh, the grandchildren. After all, they were so looking forward to some crumble pie,' said Grandma.

'Oh, I'm sure they'll get here when they can,' said Mrs Crumble turning back to her stove. Grandma Beany looked at Mr Applefield shaking her head, 'What do we do now? I thought she would go and look for them,' she whispered. Mr Applefield popped another spoonful of pie into his mouth and tried to think of another plan. Suddenly his eyes lit up and his big mop of hair stood to attention on the top of his head. Grandma Beanys eyes widened at such a sight. Mr Applefield bent across and whispered to Grandma, 'We must creep to the front door then run for our tummies!' Grandma thought for a moment. 'Hmm? Run you say,' she whispered back.

Mr Applefield nodded his head up and down so fast it made his big mop of hair wobble about like a jelly. Grandma Beany had no idea if she could even walk let alone run being so full of pie, but it did seem to be the only way they were going to get out of crumble cottage. She whispered back, 'After the count of three, we'll creep to the front door.'

'Agreed,' whispered Mr Applefield. 'One, two, three!' both stood up and very gently lifted their chairs back away from the table, and began to creep to the door. Oh, how they wanted to groan with agony at being so full, but of course they dare not make one sound. All the while, Mrs Crumble was still at her stove talking and stirring, she had not noticed her guests had opened the cottage door and were now outside. They closed the door ever so quietly behind them. With their hearts pounding like bongo drums in their ears and their full tummies, they both took one look at one another, nodded their heads and cried, 'Run like the clappers!' They had forgotten they had said run like the clappers, and there suddenly, all along the field were the clapper hands. 'Oh, no,' cried Grandma while trying really hard not to laugh at Mr Applefield, who was still trying to run with one hand holding his tummy up and the other keeping his big mop of hair from falling on his face.

'We must stop giggling,' said Grandma, but when she looked at Mr Applefield, all tangled in his own hair, rolling about laughing and hearing the hands still clapping, it just started her off again. Once they had calmed down and caught their breath, Grandma walked over to the gate and shouted, 'You can stop clapping, now we've stopped running like the clappers.'

'Okay,' said all the hands sadly so they stopped clapping, and disappeared. As for Mrs Crumble, she still had not even noticed her guests had gone.

'Well, there's nothing for it. We must get back to Blossom Top and wait for news of the children,' said Grandma.

As they were limping back like over fed canaries with huge tummies and cotton skinny legs, they could hear the flower meadow singing in the distance calling to them.

'Come sit with me in the warm sunshine, we will sing so well, our perfume you will smell, lay down in the sea of green, close your eyes and daydream.' Mr Applefield and Grandma started to walk quickly, both had no time for daydreaming today. They eventually reached Blossom Top and Mr Applefield said he knew they did not have time for a flower meadow daydream, but did Grandma think they might have time to walk through Butterfly Row instead of running, as he thought a burst of happiness would rather soothe his very large stomach and wobbly legs. Grandma Beany agreed to his request. Butterfly Row always let him go in the end. Anyone else they kept forever.

They finally reached the row and started to walk through, oh, how their nostrils quivered with pleasure at the scent of sweet lavender and buddleia bush it made them feel dizzy with happiness. It was always a glorious summer's day in Butterfly Row, even in the winter. The bees were gently buzzing while collecting their pollen; the butterflies were flying around them, displaying the most glorious colours imaginable. Grandma Beany and Mr Applefield stood gently turning around and around with arms stretched out in a golden sun dust haze of happiness. Both had the biggest smiles on their faces that you ever did see. Then the butterfly fairies came and started to crowd around them, whispering in tiny voices into their ears,

'Come with us! Come with us! We will take you there, where happiness abounds, and joy is everywhere.' Their bodies began to tingle, and their feet were lifting off the ground, when Grandma Beany shouted, 'Stop! As lovely as you are, my darlings, I have to go.' All the butterfly fairies flew aside to allow her to pass. She looked back at Mr Applefield, although she could not see him, only bright sparkles. Grandma thought she would sit for a moment, just to see if Mr Applefield should appear and before she even got comfortable, he slid right past her.

'That was truly wonderful,' said Mr Applefield, 'a joy above joy! I am feeling so much better and very happy, I must say.'

'That's wonderful,' said Grandma and they both made their way quickly back to the cottage. Grandma opened the kitchen door to a chorus of laughter and raspberries everywhere. Prunella was in a pickle and Digby door solder had come into the kitchen to find out what all the noise was about. Grandma Beany stood smiling at the sight along with Mr Applefield, both finding it very hard not to laugh themselves. Prunella saw them and cried, 'Thank goodness! You are home.' With this, the whole kitchen turned to see who she was talking to and on seeing Grandma, fell silent.

Chapter Six

'I thought you were a rabbit,' said Callie.

'So, did I,' said Jack.

'Yep, many 'ave thought that, but you would never get across Tumble Weed Farm with a rabbit. The weeds would easy win over a rabbit.'

'These spikes are what you need.,' said Skipperty and proudly showed his amazing spikes off. 'On guard!' he called and rolled into a ball, displaying very long, very shiny and very, very sharp spines.

'Wow! They are fantastic,' agreed Jack and Callie. Skipperty unrolled himself, stood upright and lent back against the tree. He let out a big sigh, nodded his head and said, 'Yep, wow! I am always thinking how amazing I am, of course you have not seen the half of me yet.'

Jack and Callie looked at each other and raised their eyebrows. 'Anyways what's your business here? ?' asked Skipperty.

'We are looking for the Spindle Webs,' said Jack, and proceeded to tell Skipperty the story so far. Whilst Jack was talking to him, Skipperty, from the corner of his eye thought he saw something move over in the grass. He casually walked a little closer, yep, he could see it clearly now, a stingle! Skipperty moved like a lightning flash and stuck his foot down on one of the stingle's arms; it screamed so loudly it made the children jump.

'Quiet! Quiet! You little devil,' said Skipperty.

'What is it?' asked Callie, 'Look at its cute little face,' she continued.

'Great Gathering Conkers!' said Jack, and with a loud crashing sound, all the conkers rushed out. Jack put his hands up to stop them, 'Not now!' he said so they all turned around feeling rather embarrassed at their shoddy entrance and marched back silently to Clobbernut. Booga Conk turned back quickly and took aim, but was swiftly grabbed by Captain Conk before he could fire any bogies. 'Yes, what is it?' asked Jack.

'This my friends, is a stingle,' said Skipperty. Callie started walking towards it, 'Ah! How cute! Please do not hurt him.'

'Do not touch him!' warned Skipperty. 'Cute you say,' he laughed. Jack became a little cross with Skipperty for laughing at his sister and promptly reminded him she was, after all a girl and he should know that girls get all mushy over cute things, and with that, Callie gave Jack a very cross look and pulled his nose.

'Ouch!' he said. 'What was that for?' Callie said nothing and continued to watch the stingle in amazement.

'Well,' said Skipperty, after he had finished laughing. 'I'll tell you this; the whole of Upside Wood will know you're coming now, thanks to this little critter.' He took his foot off the stingle's arm and as it turned to run, he gave it a sharp kick up the backside, which lifted the little blighter high into the air. It squealed loud enough for the inhabitants of Upside wood to hear.

'Oh, Skipperty, that was cruel,' said Callie looking very concerned. Skipperty laughed.

'That cute little thing, as you call it, has a sting a hundred times more powerful than a wasp and he will use it, no matter who you are, make no mistake. You'll be covered in painful red, stinking pus oozing bumps for weeks!'

'Ouch,' grimaced Jack.

'Oh,' said Callie looking at the ground and feeling rather silly.

'Right,' said Skipperty, 'we cannot waste any more time. That wood knows you are coming so we will need to hurry.' All three headed back towards the two trees, which were both very wide and very tall, with enormous branches that looked like they were disappearing into the sky. They were clothed in giant bright green leaves, the size of umbrellas.

'I can't see a farm anywhere,' said Jack.

'You will,' said Skipperty, 'You will.' They were all stood in between both trees, when Skipperty shouted, 'Uli up!' and to the children's hum dinging, all singing surprise, the trees started to bend outwards. Each tree making thunderous creaking and stretching sounds, and through the trees Jack and Callie began to see a rainbow shape of deep blue start to appear. As the trees bent outwards even more, there came such a bright blaze of yellow, it hit them right in the eyes. Skipperty pulled out two pairs of sunglasses and the children put them on. Looking straight ahead all they could see were huge thick green stems as wide as a house, and lifting their heads, and following the stems upwards, they could see the biggest most yellow sunflowers, so big it took their breath away!

'Great Gathering Conkers!' said Jack and added quickly, 'No! No! Do not come out guys. Jack was fast learning how to control his gift.

'Golden Goshes!' cried Callie, and before she could say anything else, the sparkly halo appeared and the heavenly music began to play followed by the invisible tornado whipping up her golden hair holding it above her head blowing it in all directions, and then, as if from nowhere, appeared the fat babies dancing and swirling around amongst her golden locks. Callie herself was entranced within the warm breeze and heavenly music. She herself was swaying gently and being quite carried away. Skipperty could not believe what he was seeing, so he looked over at Jack for the answer. Jack just shook his head and said.

'It just happens every time she says it, it's Callie's gift.' Still nodding his head, he added, 'It's a girl thing.'

'Hmm, it's a new one on me and I'd thought I'd seen it all,' said Skipperty. 'What use are they? Same as your, conkers, none I bet.' Skipperty began to laugh.

'Ah, they come in handy when we really need them, Skipperty, make no mistake,' replied Jack, who then shouted at Callie. Making her jump, which stopped the wind and made her hair fall back down. This unbalanced the fat babies and they started to bump into one another causing them to get angry and begin to wail. 'Get down!' Jack said to Skipperty.

'Why?' said Skipperty.

Then came the flaming arrows flying everywhere.

'Ah, that's why,' shouted Skipperty above the wailing, while quickly dodging one of the arrows which came within an inch of his whisker hair.

'CALLIE!' shouted Jack, as loud as he could.

'Sorry Jack, I was carried away there for a moment,' said Callie, thinking nothing of it and telling the fat babies to please leave.

'They're amazing, aren't they? My little devils,' said Callie smiling proudly, 'so are these sunflowers,' and she started walking towards the enormous green stems? Skipperty suddenly jumped in front of her.

'Stopperty! Stop! Stop!' he shouted. Jack ran forwards to be with Callie.

'Remember, this is Tumble Weed Farm, it doesn't have that name for nothing you know,' warned Skipperty. Then there came a rather loud groaning sound, which seemed to be coming from up above them.

'It's the sunflowers,' said Jack. The sunflowers started to wake up, aware that they had company.

'Ahhhh,' they were all sighing together causing a warm breeze to swirl downwards and brush past everyone's faces. One sunflower bent forward towards them, still groaning slightly and creaking as it bent downwards its large stem showering them in soft yellow rain.

'What is it?' asked Callie. Jack and Callie held out their hands to catch the raindrops.

'Pollen, that's what.' replied Skipperty.

'Hello, Skipperty,' said the sunflower in the smoothest, loveliest velvet sounding voice ever.

''Ello,' replied Skipperty in the roughest voice ever! The sunflower turned towards Jack and Callie and seemed to be smiling at them.

'Hello, have you come to play?' said the sunflower.

'Play? Play what?' asked Jack.

'Perfangal,' said the sunflower, and with this, all the sunflowers repeated the word as if in a whisper.

'Perfangal.' Jack and Callie turned towards Skipperty and asked what perfangal was.

'Well,' he said. 'It's a sort of game it is. You 'ave to play it to get across the field as there's no other way, but mark my words, it's not easy and can be deadly,' Skipperty continued, 'Perfangal, to those who do not know about it, is known as puff and tangle perfangal.' When the sunflowers heard the word, they all repeated it again in a whisper.

'Perfangal.'

'How do you play it, Skipperty?' Jack and Callie asked.

'Well, it's like this, one of these ' sunflowers will bend down for you to climb up on it.'

'Oh dear,' said Callie.

'Don't worry,' said Jack, 'we will be fine. It will be just like riding Dylan, your pony.' He reassured her. 'Can we ride one together?' asked Jack.

'Nope,' one each, them is the rules. Now, I will give you the rest of the rules, so listen close,' said Skipperty. 'Once yer up there, these 'ere sunflowers are going to puff you from one to the other. It'll be fun, like falling around on large fluffy clouds.'

'Sounds great,' said Callie.

'That it is,' said Skipperty.

'What's the catch, Skipperty?' asked Jack, knowing there must be one as Skipperty had said in the beginning, this was Tumble Weed Farm.

'Oh, yes, indeed, you're right to ask,' answered Skipperty.

'Once you are up so high, the rookery bridge rooks are going to see ya and they will start to crow, and once that starts it will wake Farmer Wibberly.'

'What's the problem with that?' asked Jack.

'Well, I'll tell ya the problem. He will come out of his farmhouse over yonder and them rooks, I said about, well,

47

they'll start shouting wobberly, you see,' said Skipperty. Jack and Callie looked at one another with a questioning look.

'Well, what happens when they say wobberly?' asked Callie.

'Can't you work it out?' said Skipperty.

'Er, no. Sorry,' said Jack. Skipperty let out a big sigh!

'Well, it's like this. He is called Farmer Wibberly and everyone knows, in these parts, that if you say wobberly to Farmer Wibberly, he will fall over laughing, and when that 'appens, out will come The Tangles.'

'The Tangles?' asked Jack.

'I told ya, puff and tangle, perfangal,' said Skipperty. Again, came the whisper from the sunflowers.... 'Perfangal.'

'Oh!' said Jack and Callie, both frowning and not sure if they knew what Skipperty meant or not.

'The tangles grow up from the earth under. It is a dark and mysterious world, nothing like ours. The Tangles will try to grab ya while your being puffed from one sunflower to the other and that is where I come in. Oh, and err, Mr Blow Pants, he is a mate of mine, in fact he should be ere right after I.' With that, Skipperty let out a deafening whistle the children had to cover their ears, and on Rookery Bridge all the rooks stopped what they were doing and scanned the sky with one beady eye each in deadly silence, something was coming, they just knew it! Jack, Callie and Skipperty, stood looking up for what seemed like ages.

'Should not be long now, I can hear him in the distance,' said Skipperty. Jack and Callie strained their ears trying hard to hear anything. Then.

'Callie,' Jack whispered. 'Can you hear that?' he asked. In the distance there seemed to be a rumbling, a bit like when you blow a raspberry and hum at the same time. It seemed to come and go and as it got closer, they could hear laughing, real belly laughing. Suddenly there he came zooming in.

'Landing gear! Ha ha ha ha! Landing gear, landing gear, where are you? Ha ha ha, chug chug chug,' thump skidding passed them all holding back his braces and digging into the ground with his propeller boots, went Mr Blow Pants giggling and bidding them all hello on his way by. 'I'll be back shortly! Ha ha ha!' he shouted back at them, still laughing.

'He'll crash into something in just a minute, always does,' said Skipperty.

The children watched as Mr Blow Pants disappeared into the large sunflower stems, belly laughing all the way. After about 10 minutes and a lot of shuffling around Jack and Callie watched Mr Blow Pants, emerge from a cloud of dry earth still laughing his head off. He was small, and round looking with large plump cheeks a happy moon looking face a flying hat and huge flying goggles. He walked with a waddle and seemed quite unable to stop laughing.

'Did you see that landing? Ha ha ha ha! Did you? It was Spectacular! Spot on! Blow Pants at your service. How can I help my old pal Skipperty then?'

'Blow Pants, this is Jack and Callie, they need to find the Spindle Webs, meaning a trip to Upside Wood. Mr Blow Pants scanned the children up and down through his huge flying goggles. He 'oommed' and 'ahhhhed then fell about belly laughing once again.

'Give 'im a minute,' said Skipperty, 'always laughing, aint ya, Blow Pants?'

'Always,' Blow Pants replied between chuckles.

'Perfangal, perfangal,' kept whispering the sunflowers. Getting impatient and wanting to play, they did not like being woken up for nothing.

'Jack,' said Skipperty, 'there's no time to waste; we all need to get a move on.' Jack nodded in agreement.

'Right, you two, when I say, 'game on for two', the sunflowers will bend themselves down to you and you are to move forward and grab a good hold, then up you'll go.' Callie, feeling rather nervous mistakenly said aloud, 'Golden Goshes!' She quickly slapped her hand over her mouth, but it was too late, a sparkly halo of light appeared heavenly music began to play, and the tornado of wind picked up her hair in a swirl and out came the fat babies, all having a good look around.

'Cor blimey, here we go again,' said Skipperty.

Mr Blow Pants stopped laughing immediately and removed his flying goggles, something he rarely did, just to get a better look.

'Well, I never!' he said. 'That's a sight, if ever there was one. Fat babies everywhere,' and with that Mr Blow Pants fell to the ground bouncing around with laughter. One of the fat babies not very happy with being called a "fat baby" took aim with his bow and fired. All the other fat babies clapped. It was a very good shot, right into Blow Pants bottom. He gave out a real scream then turned and pulled the arrow out patting his trousers urgently to snuff out the flames and said, 'I do not believe it! They're fat babies with weapons!' This just made him belly laugh even more, in fact, he was laughing so much and so loud, that Jack and Skipperty began to laugh too. The fat babies were furious, they all took aim with their bows and were about to fire when Callie realizing this, quickly asked them to leave, as it was a mistake she had not meant to call them. She told them they would soon to be very busy, and they must save their energy. A very serious situation awaits them. The fat babies thought for a moment then tut, tutted and gave everyone their very angriest looks and left. Mr Blow Pants just continued to fall about belly laughing once again while Skipperty got on with the job of instructing the children on the game of perfangal.

'Are you ready?' asked Skipperty.

'We are,' said Jack and Callie and together called, 'Game on!' to the sunflowers.

'Game on! Game on!' all the sunflowers whispered in their velvet tones and then began to bend forwards. The creaking and the groaning was so loud it sounded like tree trunks snapping in two and echoed loudly. Golden pollen rain was falling like snow and covering everything, and everyone. As the flower heads got closer, it began to get darker as they were so large, they were blocking out the daylight. Then all the groaning and creaking stopped and there in front of the children were two enormous sunflowers wearing very large smiles.

'Be brave, Callie,' said Jack. The children now covered in pollen grabbed on as tightly as they could to each of their sunflowers. Callie buried her face into hers, holding more tightly than she had ever held anything before. Once more, came the loud creaking and groaning sounds as the sunflowers began to make their way upright.

'Hold on, Callie,' shouted Jack as loudly as he could. Callie did not hear him; she still had her face buried deep into the sunflower's head, not daring to look!

Chapter Seven

On Rookery Bridge, the rooks were still scanning the sky with their one beady eye and staying very quiet so as not to miss anything. One of them suddenly caught sight of something racing over the bridge very fast, the rook jumped down off the side of the bridge and flew to the end to stand guard and catch whatever it was he had seen. The other rooks turned their heads to see what he was doing. Then before the something could make a dash for it and get past, the large rook whipped it up in his beak! It was the stingle Skipperty had rudely catapulted into the air earlier. The stingle squealed and squeaked and wriggled so much the rook lost grip and dropped him, all the rooks beady eyes left their sockets and rolled after the stingle, following his every move at speed. The rooks were super sure now that something big was about to happen, but they stayed on the bridge and let their beady eyes do all the work for them.

The stingle meanwhile was running his little heart out he knew the rook's beady eyes were hot on his tail! He also knew they wouldn't go all the way into Upside Wood, one because it would be hard to get past the boundary of stingle folk, and two for fear of Ethel Eye Balls and the Giddy Aunts who would be sure to steal them and add them to their collection.

As the tall trees of upside wood were looming ever closer, the daylight began to fade. He was nearly there, and with his little heart still pounding wildly in his chest, he sped up as much as his little legs could go. Finally, he fell at the foot of the line of stingles that surrounded the wood and with such a sudden stop, the beady eyes all came tumbling over him. The stingle alarm began to ring throughout, alerting all within of intruders. The rooks' beady eyes made a hasty retreat and began to roll back to Rookery Bridge and the safety of their sockets. Behind hundreds of stingles that had gathered to protect the wood stood Ethel Eye Balls and the Giddy Aunts already waiting to add the beady eyes to their collection. They actually had some very important eyes in their collection, which they were very proud to own. Once the beady eyes were back in their sockets, the rooks took flight over the Wibberly farm and began to crow loudly waking Farmer Wibberly. He came out of his cottage and the rooks began to play.

Skipperty and Mr Blow Pants were now on red alert as they knew Farmer Wibberly was out and that the rooks had started to shout wobbly making Farmer Wibberly laugh and fall, which in turn alerted the Tumble Weeds underground to rise and attack.

Jack and Callie were blissfully unaware of anything. They were far too busy being puffed from one sunflower to the other, they just could not stop laughing; both were completely yellow. It was like landing on the softest of cotton wool , in fact, softer, and once you landed, the sunflower would blow you off again and another would catch you. Perfangal seemed to be the sunflower's ball game.

Chapter Eight

'Hello, everyone,' Grandma said. 'Oh, Prunella dear, what has happened to your shade?'

'Oh, Grandma, I am so pleased to see you, I have been shade-less for hours and hours! Where have you been all this time?' cried Prunella.

'Ah, Prue, let me put your shade back for you, dear. I must say, it is rather nice to hear you say you are pleased to see me! I have never heard you say that before, Prue.'

'Yes, well, don't get excited. I shall make sure I won't need to say it again.' Prunella retorted.

Grandma laughed and walked over to the kettle to make a teapot tea and tell everyone what had happened so far.

'I'm sure it won't be long now,' boomed Mr Applefield. Grandma nodded in agreement, and sure enough, the large knocker knocked loudly, and Digby raced along the hallway. He opened the door with such excitement it nearly knocked him flying.

'Come in, come in and how do you do? It's very good to see you,' he said, with a very big grin on his face.

'Hello, Digby, old chap,' said a very tall man with a very long nose, long hair and brilliant blue eyes. He was wearing rather smart orange trousers that were too short for his legs and a very fancy orange jacket; if the sun shone on him, the reflection would blind you. There is a good reason for this, and there is a good reason why he wears two pairs of shoes.

'Hello, Tommy Two Shoes,' said Digby smiling from ear to ear. Behind Tommy came another, 'Hello, Digby. How you doing, little person? What a great little person you are. Fantastic! Marvellous! You're the best!'

'Oh, for goodness sake do shut your cake hole. By the time you stop talking, I shall have died of hunger,' said Tommy.

'Put it there, little man,' said Arthur Cake. 'Always being told to shut me cake hole!' he said and started to laugh. 'Get it? Cake hole!' Digby started to laugh too. Arthur, unable to help himself, began to sing,

'I'm a swap toad and I don't care, watch my tongue whip through the air.' As he sang, Arthur waddled along clicking his fingers to the beat. Grandma called out, 'Come in and join us, Gentlemen,' and they both did just that.

Back at the front door, there was another.

'Hello, Digby.' The voice sounded like a million of the sweetest harps playing all at the same time. Digby had to walk out a little to peer around the corner and there she was, Falandra Star, one of the most beautiful pond angels you would ever meet. She was seated on 'Horse of Course'.

'Hello,' said Digby smiling from ear to ear. His little cheeks turned a bright red. He had never seen anything or anyone more beautiful, 'Come in. Come in. Oh, please do, it is so very nice to see you.' He struggled to say.

'Ah, my sweet Digby.' Alas, I cannot, I must stay with Horse of Course and keep watch.' Ferlandra smiled a love heat smile and Digby went back inside, covered in warm pond angel glow.

'Horse of Course' is one of the Blossom Top Stallions who live on the forever grasslands. They can fly faster than the speed of sound and have hooves as large as dustbin lids; there is a good reason for this.

'You know why we are here, Grandma,' Tommy Two Shoes said.

'I do indeed.'

'We heard the rooks cry. They must be at Farmer Wibberley's,' said Arthur.

'They are,' said Grandma.

'We have a Pond Angel, outside,' but before Tommy Two Shoes could finish, Grandma and Mr Appletield both said together, 'A Pond Angel!' and went rushing out.

'Pond angels are the only ones who can speak Spindle Web,' Tommy finished to himself.

'Hello, my dear,' said Grandma, looking on in wonder.

'Hello, Grandma,' replied Ferlandra. Mr Applefield was far too stunned to boom anything he could only think how beautiful she was. On reading his mind, something pond angels are very good at, Ferlandra gave him a beautiful smile filled with love heat that covered him in warm pond angel glow.

They all followed one another back inside and began to talk of all the recent events and prepare for action. No sooner had they sat down than they heard shrill screams, and at the same time, everyone in the cottage began to shiver. The spoons started to cry, and Mr Jar was going to laugh, but thought better of it. Sultana Jar tightened her lid as did all the other jars.

Those that could ran outside to see what was going on and could not believe the sight that met them, thousands of freezlings. Falandra Star was using her pond glow shield to melt as many as she could, while Horse of Course was hoofing freezelings all over the place with his dustbin lid sized hoofers, sending them flying at least 20 or 30 at a time, but there were hundreds.

'It has started, Grandma, we must leave,' said Tommy and with that, both him and Arthur jumped upon Horse of Course with Falandra and disappeared from sight with the freezelings hot on their heels. Grandma and Mr Applefield went back in doors to reassure everyone that all will be okay hoping they were right!

Chapter Nine

The coming of the Spindle Webs.

The freezelings were freezing nearly everything in their path while chasing Horse of Course. Mrs Crumble's cooker froze right in front of her eyes she touched it, and screamed. She quickly ran outside only to find that her farm had turned white, but all the same, she still took the opportunity to scan her fields in case anyone or anything was in need of her pie.

Things were bad at Tumble Weed Farm now. The rooks were shouting, 'Wobberly, wobberly!' and crowing with laughter every time Farmer Wibberly fell, which had been three times so far and the Tumble Weeds were starting to rise. The sun flowers were still so busy playing perfangal, not even they had noticed the ground shaking, nor had their new toys, the children, who were still belly laughing being puffed from one to another turning more and more yellow with each landing. Skipperty had noticed though and shouted to Mr Blow Pants to fly in among the sunflower stems and attack the Tumble Weeds head on.

'Blow 'em 'ard! Blow Pants. Knock 'em out if you please,' shouted Skipperty. Roars of laughter started to come from Blow Pants as he revved up his boots and shot off. He whizzed around amongst the stems laughing, while delivering lethal butt clouds onto the Tumble Weeds. They recoiled in horror when the butt cloud hit their nostrils, making them loose concentration long enough for Skipperty to fire his spikes. He fired them hard and fast the Tumble Weeds started to thrash about as each spike tore into them knocking them into the sunflowers. All the commotion started to cause the sunflowers to panic and their throwing became wonky and jolty. Jack and Callie were sliding around now finding it more and more difficult to hold on. Callie, starting to fall called to Jack as loudly as she could, then suddenly, they were both in mid-air actually falling , it was an awful long way down and as they fell, it was becoming colder.

'Don't worry, Jack, I'll save you,' screamed Callie.

Then, just as she was going to say Golden Goshes, so the fat babies could fly them back down to safety. A hand grabbed hold of her arm and she bumped into Jack as the hand grabbed him too! She let out a scream as they both knocked against the soft warm body of Horse Of Course. Everyone landed safely and the children just stood looking at Horse of Course, then they spotted Arthur Cake, Tommy Two Shoes and a beautiful light being.

'In case, you're wondering, which I think you are.' Tommy said to them. 'This is Ferlandra Star, a pond angel. Ferlandra looked at the children and gave them a pond angel glow instantly making them both feel amazingly warm and safe.

Skipperty and Blow Pants had finally made the Tumble Weeds retreat. Poor Farmer Wibberly had crawled back into his farmhouse exhausted. The rooks still circled, but had noticed Horse of Course and started to fly back to the bridge.

'Skipperty, and Blow Pants, as I live and breathe I cant believe its you, said Tommy two shoes How are ya? I haven't seen you two for, er, how long now? Yep, too long, too long,' interupted Arthur. He walked over to the children.

'Arthur Cake,' he said.

'Oh, no, thank you,' said Callie, 'I'm not really hungry at the moment.' Arthur fell about laughing, as did Blow Pants. Both were on the floor giggling to blazes. Skipperty found it hard not to laugh, as did the others.

'Alright, alright,' said Tommy clapping his hands and just when they had nearly stopped laughing, Blow Pants let off a butt cloud. Arthur fell to the floor holding his tummy making hog sounds, which made Blow Pants roar with laughter even more. Skipperty raised his eyebrows so fast, they came off his head and hit Tommy Two Shoes right in the eyes before going back again. This started Tommy off giggling like a girl along with Jack and Callie, in fact, everyone was laughing even Ferlandra until the ground began to shake.

'I'd forgotten, where did the freezelings go, I wonder? They were hot on our tail,' said Tommy, 'and what is that sound?' Across the bridge at Upside Wood, the stingles were cowering. Behind the stingles, Ethel Eye Balls and the Giddy Aunts looked at each other rubbing their hands together at the thought of how many eyes they might collect. The sound grew louder, and the ground began to shake even more.

'It's the Spindle Webs! They are coming,' said Ferlandra.

'Golden Goshes!' and with that came the halo followed by the tornado wind which whipped up Callie's hair around her head and out came the fat babies, bows at the ready.

'Here we go again!' said Skipperty.

'Ah, I was wondering if you took after your mother?' said Ferlandra. 'And you, Jack. You have the Great Gathering Conkers, I believe.'

'Both, worthy opponents indeed,' said Tommy.

'You knew about these spectacles?' said Skipperty sounding surprised.

'Yes, Skips, we did, their mother had both but when she had the children, they split to protect each one and to help protect Blossom Top, as had their mother and Grandma Beany before them.' explained Tommy.

The fat babies then noticed Ferlandra and as they were also mind readers, no one else got to hear what they spoke of, but the fat babies discharged themselves from duty, much to Callie's relief, as she didn't really want the attention they brought her, just yet, as there was just too much going on.

Chapter Ten

Inside the wood, the coming of the Spindle Webs had not gone unnoticed the tree bodies were beginning to stir along with their Leafals. The cone cars with their cabbies were getting ready, so too were the moss men, things were really hotting up.

The tension was huge. Skipperty, Blow Pants, Arthur Cake, Tommy Two Shoes, Horse of Course, Ferlandra and the children, all made a line in front of the hundreds of stingles that were blocking the entrance to the wood. The ground shook harder and the hissing sound became louder. The stingles were all looking at one another nervously. Then down the middle of the line came, 'Cone car anyone? Cone car, cone car anyone? Cone car.' It was the unmistakable, breezy and happy tones of the acornetts, the cone car cabbies. Cone cars are the only way a goody can travel safely in Upside Wood. The acornettes lined up in between the stingles and the Blossom Top Gang, and with their engines switched off, the acornettes turned to their captive audience and with their little red berets and perfect white gloves, they began to wave their hands on each side of themselves, while twirling around and singing, 'You need a hug or a squeeze, just jump in one of these, ta tah!' All everyone could do was look on in awe.

'How, coney? Get it? Coney!' said Arthur.

'Ay?' said Blow Pants. Then they both said at once, 'acorny !' and immediately fell to the floor laughing, clearly they both found it funny no one else quite got it

The stingles were all looking around at each other giggling. Even the Great Gathering Conkers marched out to catch a glimpse of the acornettes. Cool Conk whistled and winked, Conkernaid showed off his karate moves and chest!

The acornettes blew the Great Gathering Conkers kisses and waved frantically, until Captain Conk appeared with a certain look that told them the time for romance was not now.

All this distraction had, but only for a moment, made everyone forget that the ground was still shaking and even harder now, the sky suddenly grew so dark, so quickly, the stingles let out a scream! The Cone Car Cabbies sped off at high speed and all in Upside Wood that were looking out, fell back into the darkness, and there in front of the Blossom Top Gang the dark cloud began to take shape or shapes, thousands of them.

'Hellos, Ferlandras 'tis goods tos sees yous ands goods tos feels yours loves. Wes knows ofs thes freezelingss freezings thes magics flowers meadows whichs musts nots dies thats iss whys wes haves comes tos finds yous,' hissed the Spindle Web queen.

'Dears queens, 'tiss goods tos sees yous agains toos. Wes wishs yous tos protects thes meadows until's thes chosens haves rids Blossoms Tops ofs thes freezelings,' replied Ferlandra in Spindleweb.

'Fires,' hissed the queen, and with this command hundreds of web bubbles started to fly towards the meadow. The spindleweb queen went on to tell Ferlandra that the freezelings were working for the infamous and deadly criminal known as, Mean Pong Bobalong a horrible and dark hearted little creature those that follow him and do his bidding are the desperate the needy the vulnerable and the greedy he loves being bad because he dose not know how to be anything else He wants the Popsy Twins freed. They were daffodiled a long time ago for many crimes. Ferlandra had just finished telling everyone what the queen had said, when a loud screeching sound echoed around them, the ground started to turn white with iceand through the line of stingles came the tree bodies full of leafals and above them circling were the freezelings.

Tree bodies were harmless when in the wood, but once out of the wood they become men equipped with leafals that let off a green foul-smelling gas that would turn you into moss men, from which you would never return to yourself.

'Stand your ground! Stand your ground!' shouted Tommy Two Shoes, removing his spare shoes, which when they hit you let off poisonous ink that turns you to stone, he took aim at the tree bodies. Blow Pants had already taken off and was letting off butt clouds everywhere holey moley they were bad ones. Arthur was taking down as many freezelings as he could manage with his toad tongue, and he could manage quite a few although he was finding it hard to swallow them as the Icey devils were getting frozen to his tongue and stayed there until they had defrosted a little then they slid down nicely and were very refreshing. Skipperty was firing his spines at speed with good aim and felled many freezlings shattering their bodies like glass. Tommy's shoes were whirling around and turning to stone tree bodies and stingles left right and centre, everyone was ducking and diving desperate to avoid the leafals gas! All the time though, it grew colder, so cold the Spindle Webs,' web bubbles began to freeze on route to the meadow, the freezelings laughed loudly. Horse Of Course and Fernanda Star had moved closer to the stingle line and were hoofing their way along knocking stingles in all directions but nothing could stop the freeze. The Spindle Webs fired more web bubbles, but no sooner were they in the air than they froze. They must retreat and move closer to the Meadow else it will be lost forever, and Blossom Top will be no more. Jack looked at Callie and said, 'We must do something!' No sooner had he said it than the Spindle Web queen called to Ferlandra, 'Ferlandras thes chosens musts calls theres protectors londlys, loudlys, and nows.'

'Jack, Callie, call your protectors now! Now!' spoke Ferlandra to their minds. Jack shouted at the top of his voice while all around was freezing.

'Great Gathering Conkers!' It echoed and the freezelings screeched even louder to each other.

Callie followed suit.

'Golden Goshes.' The freezelings started to freeze harder in anticipation at what was coming to get them.

The Gathering Conkers sprang out. Conkernald launched himself at a tree body exploding as he landed Spikey Conk fired spikes of steel and was taking down all in his path. Electra Conk and Cool Conk worked as a team electrocuting and freezing the freezelings, hundreds of them. Ultra-Conk began crushing Moss men and Tree bodies with his bare fists and Booga Conk was firing live bogies at will, some just froze on contact with the freezelings, but others had full effect on the leafals climbing into their mouths.

The Fat Babies, though there are only four, fired with tremendous speed thousands of flaming arrows taking down thousands of freezelings at a time. The war raged Tommy Two Shoes and Arthur Cake had killed many as had Skipperty and Blow Pants, but now they fell back and let the Great Gathering Conkers and the Fat Babies finish the job.

The tree bodies or what was left of them started to retreat into the wood with not a leafal left upon them. The Blossom Top Gang stopped and stood back wiping their brows and brushing down their clothes feeling exhausted.

The screeching of the freezelings finally stopped and those that could turned and left for the safety of the woods. The wounded fell prey to Ethel Eyeballs and The Giddy Aunts.

'The freezelings are beaten!' Bellowed Jack.

'How amazing are we!' shouted Callie.

'Should we take prisoners?' asked Jack and looked around at all the others. Tommy held his chin in deep thought, Arthur twirled his tongue around his fingers; something he did when thinking hard. Skipperty just carried on sharpening his spines and Mr Blow Pants had fallen asleep exhausted from letting off butt clouds in vast amounts. Ferlandra wanted to wrap them in a pond angel glow filled with love. It was up to Jack and Callie to think of something. Strangely, they both found themselves thinking repeatedly in their minds, which Falandra could hear.

'Let's be there, Let's be fair, Let's help where we can, we must protect the good from bad, so fair is what we will be what should we do, let's see. Everyone waited and watched while the freezelings cried for mercy from within the wood.

'Horse of Course, how vast is the Forever Lands?'

'They go on forever, Jack. They will never run out, not even if you travelled for a thousand light years.'

'It's settled then.' So Jack Callie and the gang went in and rescued the freezelings from Ethel Eyeballs and The Giddy Aunts who screamed and howled at losing their prey. Jack told the freezelings that the decision was to banish them to the Forever Lands never to return and they should be grateful that they had been spared. The freezelings began to freeze with relief.

'Whoa stop!' said Jack, 'I think there's been enough of that freezing thank you! You must leave now with Ferlandra and Horse of Course.' Ferlandra bid farewell to everyone, leaving a loving warm pond glow behind her, much to the joy of them all. The Blossom Top Gang agreed Jack and Callie's punishment of the freezelings had been fair after all; they were acting on another's orders. Callie ran and gave her brother a big hug and blew a kiss to her Fat Babies.

'Oh, it was nothing,' said Jack tapping his shoulder and quietly thanking the Great Gathering Conkers for saving the day. We had better catch up to the Spindle Webs and let them know their web bubbles will no longer be needed; the flower meadow and Blossom Top are once again safe from harm.

'Follow us then,' said Skipperty, 'else you'll fall off the world when we get back to the two trees and we can't 'ave the heroes of the day fall off the world, can we?' he said winking, and everyone started to laugh.

Except Ethel Eyeballs and The Giddy Aunts who walked back through Upside Wood squabbling amongst themselves. There was another who did not laugh either, he just watched from inside the darkness making new plans while still holding the night beings prisoner.